Feral Animals

Jill McDougall

Contents

Feral Animals

What Is a Feral Animal?

Feral animals are animals that live in the wild but are not **native wildlife**. Instead, these animals have moved into an environment where they do not belong and have become **pests**.

Farm animals, such as pigs, can become feral when they escape from captivity. Pets, such as cats and dogs, can also become feral when they are left to survive without help from humans.

Some animals, such as foxes, have always lived in the wild, but they become pests when they are introduced into a different environment.

Feral foxes are common in cities as well as rural areas.

Feral animals are pests in many different ways. Feral cats prey on native animals, while foxes kill **livestock**. Feral rabbits graze on vegetation that provides food and shelter for native wildlife. Some feral animals, such as wild horses, damage the environment with their hard hooves.

Feral animals are not cared for by humans, and therefore they often carry diseases. They can spread these diseases to other animals, and also to humans.

Most feral animals have few predators and will **adapt** to, and thrive in, their new environment. Often, their numbers increase rapidly.

a feral cat in the forest

Feral rabbits graze on native vegetation and crops, causing serious damage.

How Animals Become Feral

Animals become feral in ways that are sometimes surprising. Goldfish make gentle pets, but if they are released into rivers and streams, they become pests.

When goldfish live in waterways, they eat the animals and plants that native species depend upon. As they hunt, goldfish scoot along the bottom of waterways, turning the water muddy. In this way, goldfish destroy **aquatic** habitats. As a result, once goldfish arrive, many native species do not survive.

Goldfish can become giants in the wild. A goldfish found in the Vasse River in Western Australia weighed almost two kilograms.

Sometimes, animals are introduced into a new environment to control pests. However, introduced animals can become pests themselves.

Cane toads were released in Australia to eat beetles that were destroying sugar cane crops. Instead of eating the beetles, the toads mostly feed on other native insects, lizards and frogs.

N
Indian Ocean
Pacific Ocean
AUSTRALIA
Perth
Adelaide
Sydney
Key
cane toad distribution in 2021
expected future distribution
0 500 km

This map shows where cane toads live in Australia and where scientists think they will spread to in the future.

Cane toads are poisonous at all stages of their life cycle – as eggs, tadpoles, young toads and adults. Their poison kills native animals that prey on them. Even large animals, such as freshwater crocodiles, can die from eating cane toads.

Cane toads have adapted to Australia's vast distances by growing longer legs that help them travel further.

Feral camels were first introduced into Australia in the 1800s to help explorers travel through the dry inland areas of the continent. Then, during the late 1800s, thousands more camels were shipped to Australia to be used for transport. Long **camel trains** carried supplies to inland towns and sheep stations.

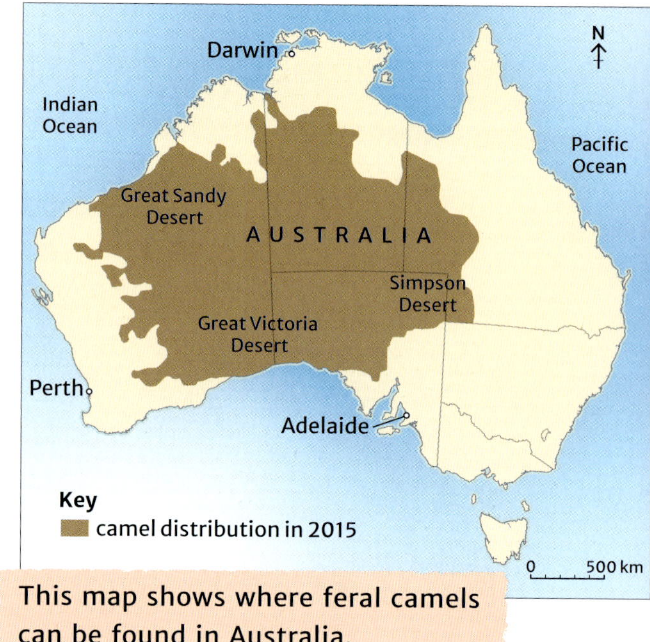

This map shows where feral camels can be found in Australia.

By the 1930s, camels were no longer useful, as goods were transported by road and rail. As a result, many camels were released into the wild and their numbers rapidly increased.

The camel trains were controlled by cameleers (people who ride camels), who came from countries such as India and Afghanistan.

Today, there are over one million feral camels throughout central Australia. The camels move in groups and eat most vegetation, including twigs and thorns. They destroy many plants that native animals depend upon for food.

Camels have wide, heavy feet. As they move about, the camels damage sand dunes and waterholes. These are important habitats for native animals and they are also important **cultural sites** for First Nations peoples.

A sign warns drivers to watch out for feral camels in central Australia.

feral camels in the Simpson Desert, South Australia

Some pests, such as fire ants, enter a new environment by accident. These pests are often carried in the **cargo** of ships.

Although they are native to South America, fire ants have become pests in Asia, North America and Australia.

a red fire ant

Fire ants are very aggressive and will swarm in large numbers to attack any animal that disturbs their nest. Their poisonous sting can kill small animals and birds.

Fire ants live underground in long tunnels. Above ground, they damage plants and can destroy entire crops.

During floods, fire ants can travel on water by linking their claws together, making a raft.

Fire ants will swarm to protect entrances to their nests.

Some marine animals become pests when they end up in oceans far from their natural habitat. Often, these animals are carried in **ballast** tanks of seawater on cargo ships. When the ship arrives in a new port, the seawater is dumped into the ocean.

Cargo ships carry seawater in ballast tanks to help them stay stable in rough weather.

The Northern Pacific seastar is a large predator that is breeding quickly in Australian waters. As its name suggests, this starfish is native to the northern Pacific Ocean – a long way from Australia.

The seastar will eat almost any animal it can capture. Scientists are concerned that, by preying on native marine life, the seastar will alter marine ecosystems.

The Northern Pacific seastar preys on native shellfish off the coasts of Tasmania and Victoria, Australia.

Feral Animals and the Ecosystem

Inside an ecosystem, living things depend on other living things for survival. When a new species, such as a pig, is introduced, it can damage or destroy the ecosystem.

Pigs are native to Africa and Asia, but live in the wild in many countries. Pigs are omnivores, which means they eat both plants and other animals. These large animals will eat almost any living things they find. These include birds, reptiles, mice, frogs and plants. As pigs search for food, they trample in waterways and uproot plants.

Scientists have found that native wildlife often cannot survive in areas where feral pigs exist.

Feral pigs have a strong sense of smell. They can detect grubs that are around seven metres underground.

Feral pigs dig for food, creating muddy areas with little vegetation and dirty water.

Animals that are not a part of the natural environment can impact the **food web** in an ecosystem.

In the 1950s, brown tree snakes were accidentally introduced to the island of Guam in the western Pacific Ocean. The tree snakes preyed on native birds, and many of these birds became extinct on the island.

Brown tree snakes are native to Indonesia, New Guinea and Australia.

The native birds were an important part of the food web in Guam's rainforests. The birds preyed on spiders, and once they were gone, the spiders had few predators. As a result, spiders are now found everywhere throughout the island's rainforests.

The rainforests of Guam are so thick with spiderwebs, people use sticks to make their way through them.

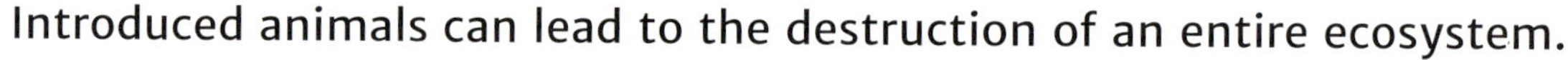

Introduced animals can lead to the destruction of an entire ecosystem.

In the 1950s, a large fish called the Nile perch was released into Lake Victoria in East Africa to boost the fishing industry. The perch is a powerful predator, and it fed on many native species, including other fish and snails. Native animals soon disappeared from the lake, and the ecosystem was changed forever.

A Nile perch swims among underwater roots.

A fisherman carries two Nile perch on a bicycle on the shore of Lake Victoria, East Africa.

Over time, thousands of people settled on the shores of the lake to fish for Nile perch.

Factories were built alongside the lake to prepare the perch for sale. Dirty wastewater from the factories poured into the lake, polluting the water. Garbage and plastic waste from people who lived near the lake added to the pollution.

Today, Lake Victoria is one of the most polluted waterways in the world, and its aquatic ecosystem has been almost wiped out.

Ibis and pigs search for food among rubbish at Lake Victoria's edge.

Feral Cats

Feral cats are a particular pest in countries such as Australia and New Zealand. They first arrived as the pets of Europeans in the 1700s.

Over time, some cats began to live in the wild, away from humans. They may have been dumped in the bush by their owner or have become lost. These animals had to learn to look after themselves.

In Australia, there could be as many as six million feral cats, and there are over two million in New Zealand. These animals can survive in many different habitats, including forests and deserts.

Feral cats are the same species as domestic cats, but they live, hunt and breed in the wild.

Cats are carnivores, which means they eat other animals to survive. They often prey on native wildlife. Scientists believe that feral cats have caused the extinction of many native animals. They report that a single feral cat will eat about 390 mammals, 225 reptiles and 130 birds in a year.

In New Zealand, one feral cat killed over 100 endangered short-tailed bats in a week.

Feral cats are also pests because they spread diseases to farm animals and pets.

Pet cats can hunt native wildlife, and in some places it is illegal for them to roam outside.

Feral Rabbits

Feral rabbits are a problem in many countries around the world. In Australia, they have possibly caused more damage than any other introduced animal.

European rabbits were brought to Australia in 1859 to be used for the sport of hunting. The rabbits were kept on a sheep farm near Geelong, Victoria, but they soon escaped and began to breed in the wild.

By 1920, there were over ten billion rabbits in Australia. They quickly spread to most parts of the country and damaged the environment wherever they went.

A female rabbit can give birth to 20 kits (baby rabbits) in a year.

Rabbit kits sleep together in a den.

Rabbits kill trees by chewing around trunks and stems. They also nibble on seedlings, which means new plants do not grow. In areas where rabbits graze, large patches of earth are often left bare. As a result, the soil blows away or is washed away in the rain.

Rabbits destroy the vegetation that native animals need for food and shelter. In some parts of Australia where there are many rabbits, animals such as bandicoots and bilbies have disappeared.

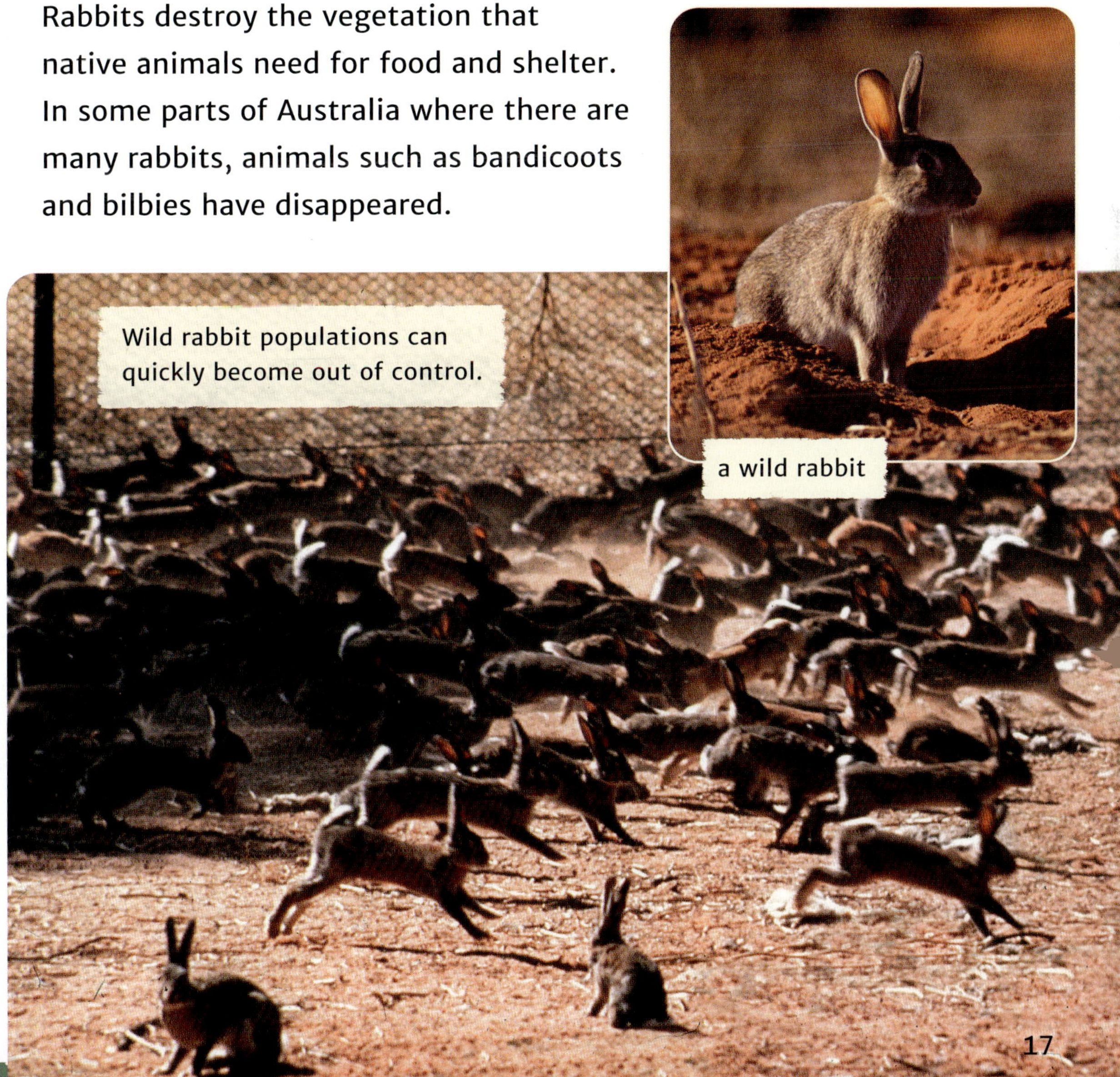

Wild rabbit populations can quickly become out of control.

a wild rabbit

How Feral Animals Are Controlled

Governments use different methods to stop dangerous new pests entering a country. Unwanted animals can arrive in planes or on board ships.

At airports and seaports, trained dogs called "sniffer dogs" are often used to locate unwanted species. Some people carry unusual animals into a country to sell as pets. If these animals escape into the wild, they can soon become pests.

Mosquitoes that carry diseases can travel from one country to another inside the cabin of a plane. To control this problem, aircraft cabins are sprayed with **insecticide**.

This baby white-cheeked gibbon was found in a suitcase in Bangkok in 2011, before it could be taken overseas.

A sniffer dog searches a piece of luggage at an airport.

When feral animals become pests, people use many different methods to control them.

In the past, animals such as rabbits were mostly controlled through trapping and shooting them. In 1950, a **virus** called myxomatosis (pronounced *mix-a-ma-toe-sis*) that causes a disease in rabbits was introduced in Australia. Since that time, different forms of this virus have been used to kill millions of feral rabbits.

Baits that contain poison are also used to control pests such as fire ants, wild pigs and feral cats.

A scientist releases the first rabbits infected with myxomatosis in a test on Wardang Island, South Australia, in 1937.

Scientists continue to find new methods to control feral animals. In remote areas, **drones** are often used to locate animals such as camels and wild cattle. Drones are also used to drop bait over large areas.

Some scientists have found a way to control cane toads using native ants. When cat food is placed near ponds, hundreds of meat ants appear. The ants eat the cat food, but they also attack young toads that emerge from the pond.

A meat ant attacks a young cane toad in the Northern Territory, Australia.

Some methods of controlling feral animals can harm native wildlife. Baits that are used to control pests may be eaten by other animals. Native animals can also be poisoned if they prey on animals that have eaten poisoned bait.

Groups such as the RSPCA (Royal Society for the Prevention of Cruelty to Animals) encourage people to use **humane** methods to control feral animals. One example is the use of soft nets to trap feral cats.

Metal cat traps with a base are another humane way to catch feral cats without harming native wildlife.

Fences can play an important role in controlling feral animals.

In Western Australia, a fence called the "rabbit-proof fence" was built in the early twentieth century. The fence stretched for 1834 kilometres, from the north of the state to the south. The government hoped that the fence would keep rabbits out of Western Australia, although some rabbits hopped into the state while the fence was being built.

The rabbit-proof fence runs through Western Australia, from its northern to southern coast.

Today, parts of this fence are still in use. Farmers keep the fence in good condition to keep out pests, such as feral goats.

The rabbit-proof fence is still in use in Western Australia.

Fences are built around **wildlife reserves** to protect native animals from predators. Inside the reserves, native wildlife can survive, thrive and breed.

Wildlife reserves in New Zealand provide a safe space for endangered animals, such as the kiwi and the giant wētā.

In 2022, **conservationists** released some eastern quolls into a large wildlife reserve in New South Wales. These animals had been extinct in the wild on the Australian mainland for over 50 years.

Conservationists hope that fenced wildlife reserves will prevent more endangered species from becoming extinct.

a giant wētā

a kiwi

an eastern quoll

Indigenous Rangers: Caring for Country

In Australia, First Nations peoples play an important role in controlling feral animals. Rangers working as a part of Indigenous ranger programs use their knowledge of Country, along with modern science, to control the spread of pests such as water buffalo, foxes and cats.

In the Kimberley region of Western Australia, rangers use drone cameras to track endangered wallabies, so they can see when they are in danger from feral cats. The cats are a threat to the black-footed rock-wallaby, or wiliji (pronounced *will-ah-chee*) as it is known by the Nyikina Mangala people. The rangers can then track down the cats to hunt or trap them.

Nyikina Mangala rangers work with Charles Darwin University drone trainers and researchers to protect native wildlife from feral cats.

In the Northern Territory, buffalo herds cause serious damage to the environment. They also destroy Aboriginal rock art and sacred sites. Indigenous rangers use computer technology to track down the herds. They are then able to move the animals away from important sites.

A turtle lays her eggs.

Teams of Indigenous rangers in Cape York, Queensland, protect turtle eggs from feral pigs. Drone cameras allow the rangers to locate turtle nests, as well as the tracks of feral pigs. By working quickly, the rangers are able to hunt the pigs before they can reach the nests.

Indigenous rangers in Cape York use a drone to locate turtle nests.

Working Towards a Pest-Free Future

Scientists, conservationists and Indigenous rangers are working together to protect natural environments from pests. Many scientists are hopeful that, if everyone works together, we can help create a pest-free future.

What Can You Do?

- Keep pet cats indoors.
- Explain to people why it is important never to dump pets.
- Report sightings of feral animals.
- Join a group that cares for native wildlife.
- Learn about feral animals in your area.
- Share the information you have learnt with others.

Indoor cats can't harm native wildlife, and they're also less likely to get injured or catch diseases.

Brumbies Should Not Be Allowed in the Alpine National Park

by Abbie, aged 11

Good morning, class.

Did you know that there are more than 5000 wild horses (known as "brumbies") in the Alpine National Park in Victoria, Australia? I think you should be just as worried about this as I am.

To begin with, the Alpine National Park was set up to protect the ecosystems in Victoria's high country. The mountain streams contain aquatic ecosystems that are easily destroyed when the brumbies trample through them. Furthermore, the mossy plants in alpine areas are very fragile. When these plants are trampled by hard hooves, they do not recover quickly.

brumby damage in the Alpine National Park

In addition to this, the brumbies actually change ecosystems. For example, when the horses trample on aquatic weeds, the weeds die. This means that fish cannot hide from the crabs that prey on them. Today, there are more crabs and fewer fish in the mountain streams because of the wild brumbies.

Furthermore, the brumbies eat vegetation that native animals feed on. As a result, animals such as the rock-wallaby cannot find enough to eat. Scientists say that in places where there are lots of brumbies, there are not many wallabies.

a brush-tailed rock-wallaby

Brumbies are beautiful animals and they deserve to be looked after. When wild horses become injured, they can die a slow and painful death. Also, when the brumbies are faced with bushfires or drought, they can die in great numbers.

Recently, some bushwalkers found a group of brumbies that had died of starvation. Surely it would be better to find new homes for these animals so they do not have to suffer!

Some people say it is cruel to remove the brumbies from the high country. However, the brumbies can be captured in humane traps that do not hurt them. Some brumbies have already been captured and are kept on farms, where they are used as **stock horses**.

In conclusion, I think the brumbies should be removed as quickly as possible. These feral horses destroy precious ecosystems and drive out native animals. Ecosystems in Victoria's high country cannot exist anywhere else, but the brumbies can.

Glossary

adapt (*verb*)	become used to something new, such as a new environment
aquatic (*adjective*)	to do with water
baits (*noun*)	foods used to attract animals
ballast (*noun*)	a heavy substance carried in a ship to keep it steady
camel trains (*noun*)	groups of camels carrying passengers and goods
cargo (*noun*)	items carried on a ship, plane, train or truck
conservationists (*noun*)	people who work to protect wildlife and the environment
cultural sites (*noun*)	places that are important to an area's culture and history
drones (*noun*)	aircraft that do not have a pilot on board and are controlled remotely
food web (*noun*)	the connected food chains that form part of an ecosystem
humane (*adjective*)	causing as little pain or distress as possible
insecticide (*noun*)	a substance that is used to kill insects
livestock (*noun*)	farm animals such as cattle and sheep
native wildlife (*noun*)	animals that belong to an environment

pests (*noun*) animals that attack or destroy crops, food, livestock or native wildlife

stock horses (*noun*) horses used to manage livestock

virus (*noun*) a type of germ that can cause disease

wildlife reserves (*noun*) protected areas for plants and animals

Index